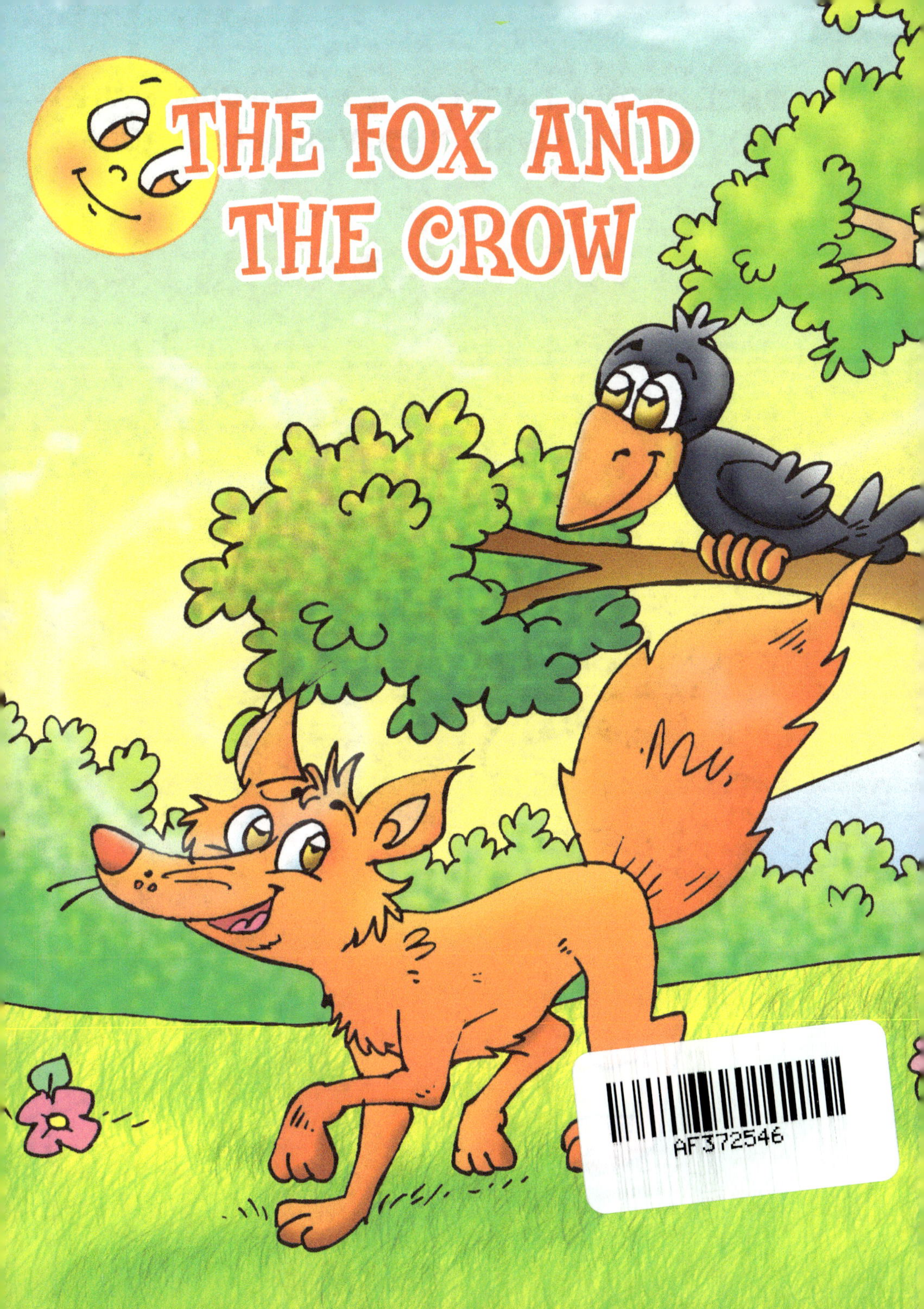

THE FOX AND
THE CROW

ONCE UPON A TIME, THERE WAS A CROW WHO LOVED TO FLY AND DISCOVER NEW PLACES.

ONE DAY, HE LANDED ON A TREE TO REST AND
WAS SURPRISED BY A FIERCE FALCON, WHO
CLAIMED IT AS HIS TERRITORY AND CHASED
THE CROW AWAY.

IMMEDIATELY, THE CROW LEFT AND
SEARCHED FOR ANOTHER TREE TO REST.

WHEN HE FINALLY FOUND A PLACE, HE CAME ACROSS TWO BOYS PLAYING AND HAVING A PICNIC. HUNGRY, THE CROW SMELLED A DELICIOUS SCENT OF CHEESE COMING FROM THE CHILDREN'S SNACK BASKET.

THE CROW THOUGHT A LOT ABOUT WHETHER HE SHOULD RISK TAKING THE CHEESE, BUT HIS STOMACH STARTED GROWLING WITH HUNGER.

SO, WHEN THE BOYS MOVED
AWAY FROM THE SNACK BASKET,
HE FLEW QUICKLY AND STOLE A
PIECE OF CHEESE.

THE CROW FLEW AWAY AS FAST AS HE COULD AND LANDED ON A TREE TO EAT THE CHEESE PEACEFULLY.

SUDDENLY, A FOX WHO WAS PASSING THROUGH THERE SMELLED THE FOOD. SHE WAS HUNGRY AND ON THE HUNT FOR SOMETHING TO EAT.

SO, THE FOX BEGAN TO THINK ABOUT HOW SHE COULD TAKE THE CROW'S CHEESE...

...SINCE THE BIRD WAS AT THE TOP OF THE TREE AND SHE COULDN'T REACH IT. SO, SHE HAD AN IDEA:

THE FOX STOPPED UNDER THE TREE AND STARTED
PRAISING THE CROW, SAYING THAT HE HAD
BEAUTIFUL FEATHERS AND WAS VERY GRACEFUL.

AFTERWARDS, SHE SAID SHE WOULD LOVE TO HEAR HIM SING, AS SHE BELIEVED CROWS HAD THE MOST BEAUTIFUL VOICE OF ALL BIRDS.

THE CROW FELT CHALLENGED AND WANTED TO PROVE THAT HE REALLY HAD A BEAUTIFUL VOICE.

HOWEVER, WHEN HE STARTED TO SING, HE OPENED HIS BEAK AND LET THE PIECE OF CHEESE FALL. IMMEDIATELY, THE FOX SNAPPED UP THE FOOD.

BEFORE LEAVING WITH THE PIECE OF CHEESE, THE FOX TOLD THE CROW THAT HE SHOULD BE SMARTER...

...AND BELIEVE LESS IN THOSE WHO FLATTER TOO MUCH, AS PRAISES ARE NOT ALWAYS SINCERE.

THE END.

www.ingramcontent.com/pod-product-compliance
Lightning Source LLC
Chambersburg PA
CBHW071307130726
47998CB00003B/1375